KU-491-568

This book is designed by

_____

Text by Emily Haynes

FOREWORD

My mother was an art teacher, and she always encouraged my siblings and me to draw and express ourselves artistically, telling us, "The arts are a noble profession." Thanks to her encouragement, all three of us went on to creative careers.

Some people talk about the ability to draw or create art as if it's a mysterious, magic power, but really it's a skill, one everyone has from birth, and one anyone can develop by practicing. Like anything else, the more you do it, the better you'll get!

Of course, the world needs people with all sorts of different interests and skills. But no matter what you do, keep drawing and making space for your artistic side! I promise that it will help you observe more keenly, appreciate the beauty of the world around you more fully, and think more creatively your whole life long.

John Lasseter

INTRODUCTION

This book was created when Cooper Hewitt, Smithsonian Design Museum invited Pixar Animation Studios to put on an exhibition about design and how it relates to storytelling. The exhibition explores how three tools of the Pixar design process—*research*, *iteration*, and *collaboration*—ultimately contribute to the success of a film's story. Now it's your turn to explore these principles—and have a lot of fun along the way.

Many people who visit Cooper Hewitt ask the same question: what is design? One answer is that design is art with a purpose. Pixar artists, animators, and other collaborators believe that the purpose of every design decision is to support the story they're telling. By making a character appealing, or a world or environment believable, Pixar is one step closer to entertaining its audience.

All designers use special tools to do their work. Pixar uses those three main tools I mentioned above—research, iteration, and collaboration—to develop its stories. Research is when you look to the rest of the world to help inspire your own work. Iteration can mean playing with different colors and shapes to create your own characters and worlds. And collaboration is when you play and work with others to help tell a story. These are the tools that designers of many stripes—from book illustrators to comic artists, graphic designers to filmmakers—use to develop stories. And now these are your tools as well.

Designing a Pixar film may seem different from designing a chair or a pair of sneakers, but they all have something in common. By making certain design decisions, you determine what kind of "story" your film or chair or sneakers are going to tell. Is it loud and vibrant? Or quiet and subdued? Sleek and modern? Or slow and old-fashioned? In these pages, you can think like a designer, looking at colors and shapes, characters and worlds in new ways—and hopefully you'll be inspired to tell stories of your own.

Michael Bierut

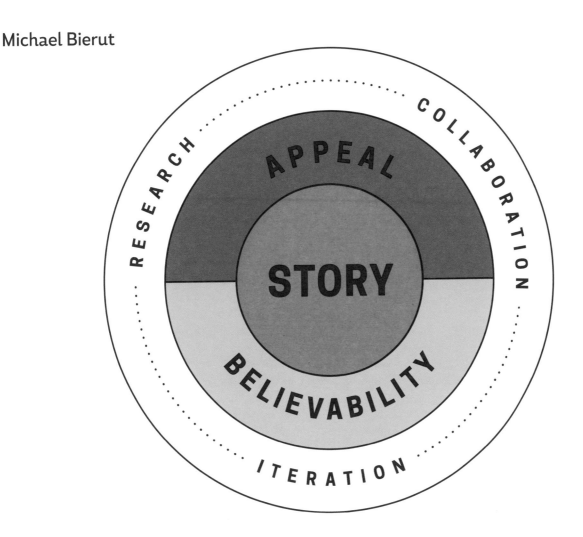

THE PIXAR STORIES

The inspiring ideas of the Pixar designers and artists featured in these pages will stir your imagination about designing a character, object, color scheme, or location. It's okay if you haven't seen every Pixar film—you don't need to know the details of the stories to have fun with these activities. What kind of story do you want to tell? What kind of world do you want to design? Dive into this book and see where your imagination can lead you.

In case you need a refresher, here are summaries of the Pixar films.

Toy Story
Ever wonder what toys do when people aren't around? *Toy Story* answers that question with a fantastic, fun-filled journey viewed through the eyes of two rival toys—Woody, the lanky, likable cowboy, and Buzz Lightyear, the fearless space ranger.

A Bug's Life
Flik is an independent-thinker ant and inventor. After one of his inventions goes terribly wrong, he embarks on a mission to help save his colony from a gang of freeloading grasshoppers. But when the group of "warrior bugs" that Flik recruits turns out to be a bumbling circus troupe, he must believe in himself and his inventions to save Ant Island once and for all.

Toy Story 2
Buzz, Woody, and their friends are back as Andy heads off to Cowboy Camp, leaving his toys on their own at home. Things shift into high gear when an obsessive toy collector named Al McWhiggin, owner of Al's Toy Barn, kidnaps Woody. Andy's toys mount a daring rescue; Buzz meets his match; and Woody has to decide where he truly belongs.

Monsters, Inc.

There's a reason why there are monsters in children's closets—scaring them is their job. Monsters, Inc., is the most successful scream-processing factory in the monster world, and there is no better Kid Scarer than James P. Sullivan (Sulley). But when Sulley accidentally lets a human girl, Boo, into Monstropolis, life turns upside down for him and his buddy, Mike.

Finding Nemo

In the colorful and tropical waters surrounding the Great Barrier Reef, a clownfish named Marlin lives with his only son, Nemo, who is eager to explore the mysterious reef. When Nemo is unexpectedly taken far from home, Marlin finds himself the unlikely hero on an epic journey to rescue his son.

The Incredibles

It takes a will of steel to hide your superhero talents from a world that needs you but no longer appreciates what you can do. Battling a bulging belly and a boring job, Mr. Incredible—Bob Parr—longs for the days of upholding law and order while he and his superhuman family try to fit in with their "normal" life. When the family uncovers a diabolical plan, they must come together with their respective strengths to save the day.

Cars

Aspiring champion race car Lightning McQueen is on the fast track to success, fame, and everything he's ever hoped for—until he takes an unexpected detour on dusty Route 66. His have-it-all-now attitude is challenged when a small-town community that time forgot shows McQueen what he's been missing in his high-octane life.

Ratatouille

A rat named Remy dreams of becoming a great chef, despite his family's wishes and the obvious problem of being a rat in a decidedly rodent-phobic profession. Remy's passion for cooking soon sets into motion a hilarious and exciting "rat race" that turns the world of Paris upside down.

WALL•E

What if mankind had to leave Earth and somebody forgot to turn off the last robot? After hundreds of years, WALL•E finally meets another robot, named EVE. EVE comes to realize that WALL•E has stumbled upon the key to the planet's future, and races back to space to report to the humans. WALL•E chases EVE across the galaxy, and many adventures follow.

Up

Carl Fredricksen, a seventy-eight-year-old balloon salesman, is not your average hero. When he ties thousands of balloons to his house and flies away to the wilds of South America, he fulfills his lifelong dream of adventure. After Carl discovers an eight-year-old stowaway named Russell, this duo soon finds itself on a hilarious journey in a lost world filled with surprises.

Toy Story 3

As Andy prepares to depart for college, Buzz, Woody, and the rest of his loyal toys are worried about their uncertain future. This comical adventure finds them in a room full of tots who can't wait to get their sticky fingers on these "new" toys. It's pandemonium as they all try to stay together, ensuring that "no toy gets left behind."

Cars 2

Star race car Lightning McQueen and tow truck Mater take their friendship to exciting new places when they head overseas to compete in the first-ever World Grand Prix to determine the world's fastest car. But the road to the championship is filled with potholes and detours when Mater gets caught up in an adventure of his own: international espionage.

Brave

Since ancient times, stories of epic battles and mystical legends have been passed through the generations across the rugged and mysterious Highlands of Scotland. In *Brave*, the courageous Merida runs into trouble when she accidently transforms her mother into a bear, and they must escape into the wilderness to set things right.

Monsters University

Mike Wazowski and James P. Sullivan are an inseparable pair, but that wasn't always the case. When these two mismatched monsters first met, they couldn't stand each other. *Monsters University* reveals how Mike and Sulley overcame their differences to become the best of friends.

Inside Out

Growing up can be a bumpy road, and there's no exception for Riley, who is uprooted from her Midwest life when her father starts a new job in San Francisco. Like all of us, Riley is guided by her Emotions—Joy, Fear, Anger, Disgust, and Sadness. The Emotions live in Headquarters, the control center inside Riley's mind, from which they advise her through everyday life.

COLORS

How are colors selected when designing a character or scene? How do they make you feel? From Merida's red hair in *Brave* to the blue of Andy's wallpaper in *Toy Story*, the colors in Pixar's films were chosen after much exploration. Let's see how you use color in your own designs.

The *Inside Out* filmmakers spent a lot of time thinking about what colors our emotions are. They ended up deciding that anger is red and disgust is green.

What colors best express your emotions? What color is joy? Sadness? Fill this page with the colors that show how you feel.

Mike Wazowski wasn't always bright green and smooth. The Pixar artists explored several different colors and patterns for him. Try out your own ideas here. What happens if you change the color of his skin? Or the pattern? Or give him fur or horns? How do the different designs change his personality?

The artists who developed the look and feel of *Brave* were inspired by traditional Scottish patterns and colors, resulting in original designs, including this one of thistles and thorns. Fill in the pattern with the colors you think work best.

The artists who worked on the Evil Emperor Zurg in *Toy Story 2* explored many different colors for his armor before settling on purple, black, and red.

The reef from *Finding Nemo* looks very different in black and white. Add some colorful fish to this scene.

Tuck and Roll, the twin pill bugs in *A Bug's Life*, are quite the jokesters. Color in this sketch of Roll to suit his circus job!

In *Monsters Inc.*, Mike and Sulley make Boo's monster costume from furniture fabric. What kind of fabric would you use? Color it using something from your home as inspiration.

The red corner, door, and chair in this abstract painting from *The Incredibles* add tension and depth to the scene—they draw your eye to the door on one side and to Mr. Incredible on the other, making a connection between the two that leads to the question "What might happen next?"

What other parts of the illustration might you color in to change the mood of the scene?

The Cars artists came up with an endless variety of car models and colors. Help them out by exploring a few different paint jobs for this character.

SHAPES

What shape is a monster? Or a pair of glasses? Deciding on the shape of a character or object is an important part of the design process. Use these iconic Pixar designs to explore the world of shapes.

In *The Incredibles*, Edna Mode's large, round glasses are an important part of her bold character.

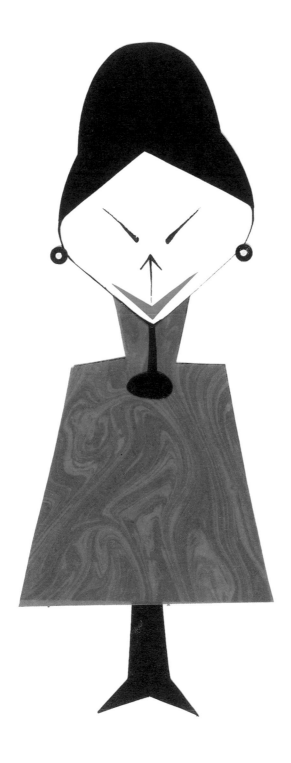

Mum-Bear in *Brave* was designed to match her human form—she is feminine and curvy, just like the queen.

28

Fergus is broad and muscular. What shape would his bear form be?

When Joy, Sadness, and Bing Bong go into the Abstract Thought building in *Inside Out*, they transform into simple, flat shapes.

Imagine that Fear, Disgust, and Anger are there as well.
What would their shapes look like?

Sometimes characters and worlds can be illustrated with very simple shapes, like in this scene with Mr. Incredible and Edna Mode. Pick one of your favorite photographs and use simple shapes to draw what is happening in the photo.

In this piece of art for *Monsters University*, Sulley, Mike, and friends are drawn using just their outlines. Can you draw a monster using only its outline? Does it still look like a monster?

The artist who worked on Rosie, the black widow spider in *A Bug's Life*, explored several different hairstyles before choosing her elegant updo.

Give her a few styles of your own and see how each changes her character.

What would a duck truck look like? Or a mouse car? Is there another animal that might inspire a cool car or truck? Design and draw it!

Can you draw someone you know in the same style—
with no curved lines?

Art is one of the odder-looking monsters in *Monsters University*—and that's saying a lot! What kind of chair would he use? Try designing one that would fit his unique shape.

CHARACTERS

From monsters to robots and bugs to rats, the
filmmakers and artists at Pixar have invented an
astounding range of beings. All of that character
design took lots of research, collaboration, and
imagination. Practice some of those skills while
creating your own designs!

Brave's Merida has very curly red hair that fits her bold personality, but curls can come in many different forms—for example, tight, loose, short, or long.

In *Cars*, Mater is a rusty old truck—he needs a fresh paint job! What do you think he looked like when he was brand new?

The cockroach in *WALL•E* is not your average bug—he is tough and expressive. And he has a pair of antennae that adds to his personality. Design your own cockroach with antennae to match its sense of adventure.

Dean Hardscrabble of *Monsters University* needs a new scary design. Draw the rest of her body.

Woody lost his cowboy hat! What else might he wear on his head? A box? A crown? Give him a new and silly look.

The artists working on *Up* explored numerous ideas for the design of Kevin, the flightless bird—who happens to be a girl! She is a goofy, oversized bird.

What kind of bird would you design?
Draw four different versions.

EVE in *WALL•E* is a hardworking probe droid, searching for signs of life on an empty planet.

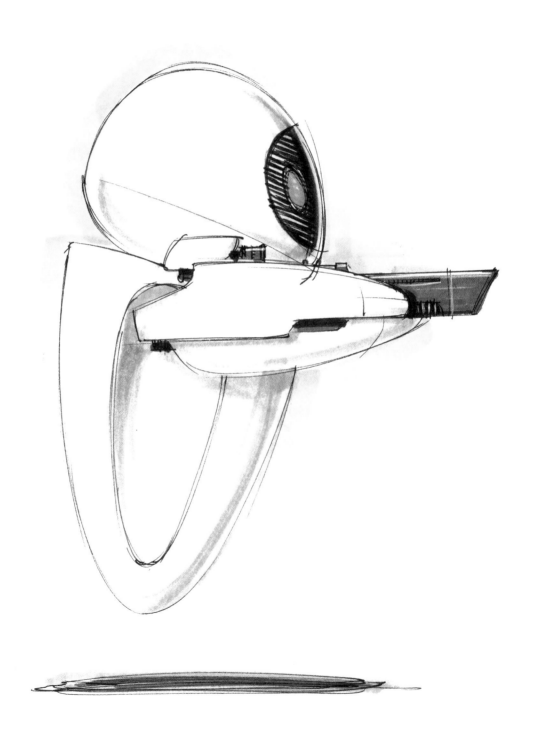

Imagine that she has just discovered an alien intruder! What does it look like? Is it armed and dangerous? Or friendly and peaceful? Design the creature EVE is aiming at with her plasma gun.

The artists working on *Monsters, Inc.* came up with a variety of monster designs. What kind of monster would you add to this lineup?

Dory from *Finding Nemo* has a very poor memory. She just met a giant fish with seven fins and rainbow stripes. She really likes him, but she's afraid she won't remember him the next time they meet. Draw a sketch of her colorful new friend so she doesn't forget what he looks like!

54

Details can really define a character, like in these sketches from *Monsters University*. Add some faces and hair—or horns!—to the unfinished monsters on this page.

Anton Ego, the food critic in *Ratatouille*, does not like the food he has been served. Draw the meal that is on his plate.

WORLDS

From a sweeping vista to the arrangement of a character's bedroom, the setting of a story—and what that world looks like—is an important design decision. The worlds in Pixar's films range from the dark and damp sewers of Paris to the bright headquarters of emotions inside an eleven-year-old girl's mind—let's see what kinds of worlds you can design!

WALL•E is the custodian of the last plant on Earth.
What will his garden look like when he finally finds
a home for it?

Carl's house in *Up* is surrounded by skyscrapers.
What kind of house would you design to fit between
these two skyscrapers?

The buildings in *Cars 2* have been "Car-ified"—designed using car parts and accessories. This bridge illustration uses tires, head lamps, and grilles for some of the structural elements.

Try designing a Car-ified house.
What features would it have?

The setting for *The Incredibles* is inspired by 1960s America. The family's house is an example of one of the popular architectural design styles of that time—midcentury modern—which features flat roofs, sharp corners, and lots of windows.

Remy, *Ratatouille*'s rat hero, loves fruit! What other kinds of tasty fruit might he want? Draw a fruit-filled bowl of temptations for him.

What is Bob Parr from *The Incredibles* watering?
A garden? His lawn? Design the world around him.

The buildings in *Monsters, Inc.* were designed
with monster details—horned roofs, monster-eye
windows, and spiky columns.

Design your own monster-themed skyscraper.

Build a world around him. What's on fire
that he needs to put out?

Frozone, Mr. Incredible's best friend, can turn the world around him to ice. Draw his superpower in action!

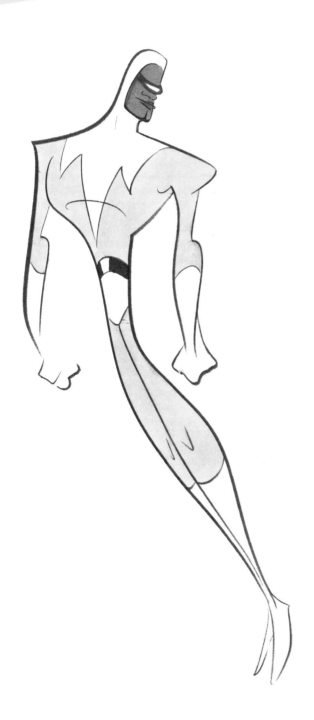

YOUR STORIES

At Pixar, design always supports a film's story, from the style of a character's hair to the color used to design a villain's lair. Look back at the colors, shapes, characters, and worlds you've created, and see what kinds of stories they might inspire when we combine them! You won't be re-creating what happens in the films here—this is an opportunity to write an entirely new story. If you need help with the writing, this is a great chance to try something the artists at Pixar practice all the time—collaboration. Find someone who can help with the words and get to work!

Take a look at the *Incredibles* art you colored in on pages 22 and 23. Imagine that the version of Woody you designed on page 47 comes through the door. What does Woody say? How does Mr. Incredible feel? Describe the scene.

Imagine that the Fergus bear you drew on page 29 wakes up in the *Incredibles* house you designed on pages 62 and 63. There's a knock on the front door. Who is it? What happens next?

The Kevin bird you sketched on page 49 lives in the *WALL•E* garden you created on page 58. What happens when the bird and robot meet for the first time?

Imagine that the monster you drew on page 52 is Anton Ego's waiter. What does Ego say about the dinner he's been served on page 56? How does the monster respond?

The Evil Emperor Zurg you designed on page 17 is in a battle with the character that EVE is blasting on page 51. How does the battle play out?

What if the character you created on page 39 lives in the building you designed on page 67. Imagine that he or she has just gotten up in the morning and sees the cockroach from page 45. What happens next?

ART CREDITS

In some cases, original artwork has been modified to suit the activity within this book.

Page 2: Woody and Buzz, *Toy Story*, 1995; Bob Pauley; Marker and pencil on paper; 20.3 x 24.1 cm (8 x 9.5 in)

Page 3: Radiator Springs Curio Shop, *Cars*, 2006; Nat McLaughlin; Pencil on paper; 27.9 x 43.2 cm (11 x 17 in)

Page 6: Carl and Russell at Paradise Falls, *Up*, 2009; Daniel Arriaga; Digital painting

Pages 7–10: *Toy Story*: Buzz, 1995; Bob Pauley; Pencil on paper; 35.2 x 27.6 cm (13.875 x 10.875 in) • *Toy Story 2*: Jessie Color Study, Toy Story 2, 1999; Jim Pearson, Marker and pencil on paper; 21.6 x 27.9 cm (8.5 x 11 in) • *Monsters, Inc.*: Mike Wazowski, 2001; Jason Deamer; Pencil on paper; 26.7 x 33 cm (10.5 x 13 in) • *Finding Nemo*: Nemo, 2003; Dan Lee; Marker on photocopy; 43.2 x 27.9 cm (17 x 11 in) • *Cars*: Lightning McQueen, 2006; Bob Pauley; Mixed media on paper; 43.2 x 27.9 cm (11 x 17 in) • *Toy Story 3*: Lotso, 2010; Daniel Arriaga; Digital painting over scanned marker and pencil on paper; 31.8 x 43.2 cm (12.5 x 17 in) • *Cars 2*: Mater Disguise: Materhosen, Cars 2, 2011; Jack Chang; Digital paint over character render • *Monsters University*: Sulley, 2013; Ricky Nierva; Ink and watercolor on paper; 26 x 15.2 cm (10.25 x 6 in) • All other art as credited in following sections.

COLORS

Section opener: Sullivan Fur Pattern Studies, *Monsters, Inc.*, 2001; Tia W. Kratter, maquette by Jerome Ranft; Mixed media on board; 26.7 x 28.6 cm (10.5 x 11.125 in)

Page 12: Anger, *Inside Out*, 2015; Chris Sasaki; Marker, pencil, and correction fluid on paper; 27.9 x 21.6 cm (11 x 8.5 in) • Disgust, *Inside Out*, 2015; Chris Sasaki; Pencil and marker on paper; 27.9 x 43.2 cm (11 x 17 in)

Page 14: Mike Color Study, *Monsters, Inc.*, 2001; Ricky Nierva; Marker and pencil on photocopy; 21.6 x 27.9 cm (8.5 x 11 in)

Page 15: Thistle Celtic Knot, *Brave*, 2012; Tia W. Kratter; Digital painting

Pages 16, 17, and 76: Zurg Color Study, *Toy Story 2*, 1999; Randy Berrett; Pencil on photocopy; 43.2 x 27.9 cm (17 x 11 in)

Pages 18–19: Home reef, *Finding Nemo*, 2003; Nelson Bohol; Marker and pencil on paper; 27.9 x 43.2 cm (11 x 17 in)

Page 20: Tuck and Roll Model Packet, *A Bug's Life*, 1998; Dan Lee; Pencil on paper; 26.7 x 33 cm (10.5 x 13 in)

Page 21: Boo in Costume, *Monsters, Inc.*, 2001; Jason Deamer; Pencil on paper; 31.7 x 26.7 cm (12.5 x 10.5 in)

Pages 22–23, and 72: Edna Mode (aka "E") House, *The Incredibles*, 2004; Teddy Newton; Collage on board; 22.2 x 47.6 cm (8.75 x 18.75 in)

Page 24: Flo Wing Study, *Cars*, 2006; Bob Pauley; Photocopy of marker and pencil on paper; 27.9 x 43.2 cm (11 x 17 in)

SHAPES

Section opener and page 32: Edna Mode (aka "E") House, *The Incredibles*, 2004; Teddy Newton; Collage on board; 12 x 20.3 cm (4.75 x 8 in)

Pages 26 and 27: Edna Mode (aka "E"), *The Incredibles*, 2004; Teddy Newton; Mixed media on paper; 38.7 x 23.2 cm (15.25 x 9.125 in)

Page 28: Queen Elinor, *Brave*, 2012; Matt Nolte; Pencil on paper; 29.8 x 20.3 cm (11.75 x 8 in) • Mum Bear, *Brave*, 2012; Matt Nolte; Pencil on paper; 27.9 x 43.1 cm (11 x 17 in)

Pages 29 and 73: King Fergus, *Brave*, 2012; Carter Goodrich; Pencil on paper; 34.3 x 27.9 cm (13.5 x 11 in)

Page 30: Abstract Joy, *Inside Out*, 2015; Albert Lozano; Grease pencil and marker on paper; 27.9 x 21.6 cm (11 x 8.5 in) • Abstract Sadness, *Inside Out*, 2015; Albert Lozano; Grease pencil and marker on paper; 27.9 x 21.6 cm (11 x 8.5 in) • Abstract Bing Bong, *Inside Out*, 2015; Albert Lozano; Grease pencil and marker on paper; 27.9 x 21.6 cm (11 x 8.5 in)

Page 31: Mind Emotions, *Inside Out*, 2015; Chris Sasaki; Digital painting

Page 33: OK Fraternity Shape Exploration, *Monsters University*, 2013; Ricky Nierva; Marker on paper; 27.9 x 43.2 cm (11 x 17 in)

Pages 34 and 35: Rosie Hair Styles, *A Bug's Life*, 1998; Dan Lee; Ink, pencil, and correction fluid on photocopy; 26.7 x 33 cm (10.5 x 13 in)

Page 36: Evolution of the Cow-to-Tractor, *Cars*, 2006; Jay Shuster; Pencil on paper; 27.9 x 43.2 cm (11 x 17 in)

Page 38: Carl, *Up*, 2009; Lou Romano; Digital painting

Page 40: Art, *Monsters University*, 2013; Ricky Nierva; Marker on paper; 27.9 x 41.9 cm (11 x 16.5 in)

CHARACTERS

Section opener: Bing Bong, *Inside Out*, 2015, Chris Sasaki; Pencil and watercolor on paper; 27.9 x 43.2 cm (11 x 17 in) • Tuck and Roll Model Packet, *A Bug's Life*, 1998; Dan Lee; Pencil on paper; 26.7 x 33 cm (10.5 x 13 in) • Slinky Dog, *Toy Story*, 1995; Bob Pauley; Pencil on paper; 29.2 x 33 cm (11.5 x 13 in) • Emile with Sausage, *Ratatouille*, 2007; Carter Goodrich; Pencil on paper; 41.9 x 35.6 cm (16.5 x 14 in) • Dean Hardscrabble, *Monsters University*, 2013; Dan Scanlon; Pencil on paper; 20 x 12.7 cm (7.875 x 5 in) • Lightning McQueen, *Cars*, 2006; Bob Pauley; Pencil on paper; Dimensions unknown • Boo in

Costume, *Monsters, Inc.*, 2001; Jason Deamer; Pencil on paper; 31.7 x 26.7 cm (12.5 x 10.5 in) • Merida, *Brave*, 2012; Tony Fucile; Pencil on paper; Dimensions unknown • Dug, *Up*, 2009; Tony Fucile; Pencil on paper; 36.7 x 31.8 cm (10.5 x 12.5 in) • King Fergus, *Brave*, 2012; Carter Goodrich; Pencil on paper; 34.3 x 27.9 cm (13.5 x 11 in) • Mum Bear, *Brave*, 2012; Matt Nolte; Pencil overlay on digital print; 34.3 x 43.2 cm (13.5 x 17 in) • WALL•E, *WALL•E*, 2008; Jason Deamer; Marker on paper; 21.6 x 17.8 cm (8.5 x 7 in) • Kevin, *Up*, 2009; Daniel López Muñoz; Pencil on paper; 27.9 x 43.2 cm (11 x 17 in) • Flo Wing Study, *Cars*, 2006; Bob Pauley; Photocopy of marker and pencil on paper; 27.9 x 43.2 cm (11 x 17 in)

Pages 42 and 43: Merida, *Brave*, 2012; Steve Purcell; Acrylic and pencil on paper; 30.5 x 22.9 cm (12 x 9 in)

Page 44: Mater, *Cars*, 2006, Bob Pauley; Pencil on paper; Dimensions unknown

Pages 45 and 77: Cockroach, *WALL•E*, 2008; Jason Deamer; Marker on paper; 27.9 x 43.2 cm (11 x 17 in)

Page 46: Dean Hardscrabble, *Monsters University*, 2013; Jason Deamer; Ink and marker on paper; 27.9 x 21.6 cm (11 x 8.5 in)

Page 47: Woody, *Toy Story*, 1995; Bud Luckey; Pencil on paper; 21.6 x 27.9 cm (8.5 x 11 in)

Page 48: Kevin, *Up*, 2009; Daniel López Muñoz; Pencil and correction fluid on paper; 43.2 x 27.9 cm (17 x 11 in) • Kevin and Egg, *Up*, 2009; Ricky Nierva; Marker and pencil; 27.9 x 21.6 cm (11 x 8.5 in); also on page 74 • Kevin, *Up*, 2009; Daniel López Muñoz; Pencil on paper; 27.9 x 43.2 cm (11 x 17 in)

Page 50: EVE, *WALL•E*, 2008; Jason Deamer; Ink and marker on paper; 27.9 x 21.6 cm (11 x 8.5 in)

Page 52: Background Monster Textures and Colors, *Monsters, Inc.*, 2001; Tia W. Kratter; Acrylic on board; 38.1 x 50.8 cm (15 x 20 in)

Page 53: Dory, *Finding Nemo*, 2003; Ralph Eggleston; Marker and pencil on photocopy; 27.9 x 43.2 cm (11 x 17 in)

Page 54: Horst, *Ratatouille*, 2007; Carter Goodrich; Pencil on paper; 48.3 x 33 cm (19 x 13 in)

Page 55: Background Monsters, *Monsters University*, 2013; Jason Deamer; Marker on paper; 21.6 x 27.9 cm (8.5 x 11 in)

Pages 56 and 75: Ego, *Ratatouille*, 2007; Carter Goodrich; Pencil on paper; 55.9 x 38.1 cm (22 x 15 in)

WORLDS
Section opener: Sequence Pastel: Jellyfish, *Finding Nemo*, 2003; Ralph Eggleston; Pastel on paper; 15.2 x 20.3 cm (6 x 8 in)

Page 58: WALL•E, *WALL•E*, 2008; Jason Deamer; Marker on paper; 21.6 x 17.8 cm (8.5 x 7 in)

Page 59: Carl's House, *Up*, 2009; Don Shank; Digital painting

Page 60: Bridge Model Packet, *Cars 2*, 2011; Armand Baltazar; Digital paint over reproduction of pencil on paper

Pages 62–63: Parr Home, *The Incredibles*, 2004; Scott Caple; Marker and pencil on paper; 27.9 x 43.2 cm (11 x 17 in)

Page 64: Remy in the Kitchen, *Ratatouille*, 2007; Robert Kondo; Digital painting

Page 65: Bob Color Study, *The Incredibles*, 2004; Tony Fucile, color by Bryn Imagire; Digital painting

Page 66: Monster City, *Monsters, Inc.*, 2001; Lou Romano; Gouache and pencil on paper; 14.6 x 23.5 cm (5.75 x 9.25 in)

Page 68: Red, *Cars*, 2006; Bob Pauley; Marker and pencil on paper; 27.9 x 43.2 cm (11 x 17 in)

Page 70: Frozone, *The Incredibles*, 2004; Teddy Newton; Marker and pencil on paper; 27.9 x 21.6 cm (11 x 8.5 in)

YOUR STORIES
Section opener: My Adventure Book, *Up*, 2009; Craig Foster and Elie Docter; Digital painting

Page 80: Bing Bong, *Inside Out*, 2015, Chris Sasaki; Pencil and ink on paper; 27.9 x 43.2 cm (11 x 17 in)

Front cover:
Alien Model Packet, *Toy Story*, 1995; Bob Pauley; Pencil on paper; 21.6 x 35.6 cm (8.5 x 14 in) • Mike, *Monster's University*, 2013; Ricky Nierva; Marker on paper; 35.6 x 27.9 cm (11 x 8.5 in) • All other art as previously credited.

Back cover:
Miles Axelrod, *Cars 2*, 2011; Jay Shuster; Digital painting • Dug, *Up*, 2009; Albert Lozano; Marker on paper; 26.7 x 33 cm (10.5 x 13 in) • Dot, *A Bug's Life*, 1998; Bob Pauley; Marker and pencil on paper; 35.6 x 27.9 cm (11 x 8.5 in) • Tuck and Roll, *A Bug's Life*, 1998; Bud Luckey; Pencil on paper; 27.9 x 35.6 cm (8.5 x 11 in) • Seagulls, *Finding Nemo*, 2003; Andrew Stanton; Marker on paper; 15.9 x 27.9 cm (6.25 x 8.5 in) • Train of Thought, *Inside Out*, 2015; Daniel Holland; Watercolor and ink on paper; 35.6 x 43.2 cm (11 x 17 in) • Anger, *Inside Out*, 2015; Albert Lozano; Collage and ink on board; 37.1 x 27.9 cm (14.625 x 8.5 in) • Background Monster, *Monster's University*, 2013; Albert Lozano; Collage on board; 38.1 x 50.8 cm (15 x 20 in) • Squishy, *Monster's University*, 2013; Jason Deamer; Ink, marker and pencil on paper; 35.6 x 27.9 cm (11 x 8.5 in) • Elastigirl Gag, *The Incredibles*, 2004; Teddy Newton; Marker on paper; 27.9 x 35.6 cm (8.5 x 11 in.) • Syndrome, *The Incredibles*, 2004; Teddy Newton; Collage on paper; 40 x 26 cm (15.75 x 10.25 in) • All other art as previously credited.

ACKNOWLEDGEMENTS

Books often take a village to manage and complete the various stages of development and publication, and this one is no exception. Thankfully, some incredibly talented and insightful folks populate this village! Huge thanks go out to Andy Dreyfus, Brianne Gallagher, Rebecca Hisiger, Maren A. Jones, Elyse Klaidman, Michelle Moretta, Shiho Tilley, and Melissa Woods at Pixar Animation Studios; Pamela Horn, Matthew Kennedy, Kim Robledo-Diga, and Cara McCarty at Cooper Hewitt; Kelli Chipponeri and Daria Harper at Chronicle Books; Glen Nakasako at Smog Design; and Emily Haynes at BluePen Agency.

John Lasseter is a two-time Academy Award®-winning director, chief creative officer at Walt Disney and Pixar Animation Studios, and principal creative officer at Walt Disney Imagineering. He directed *Toy Story*, *A Bug's Life*, *Toy Story 2*, *Cars*, and *Cars 2*.

Michael Bierut is a graphic designer, design critic, author, and educator. Bierut is responsible for leading a team of graphic designers who create identity design, environmental graphic design, and editorial design solutions. He has won hundreds of design awards and his work is represented in several permanent museum collections. Bierut's publications include *How to* (2015) and *Seventy-nine Short Essays on Design* (2012).

Emily Haynes is an editor, author, and publishing consultant with more than fifteen years in the book business under her belt. In 2015, she started her own editorial services company, BluePen Agency (www.bluepenagency.com). She lives in Oakland, California, with her fiancé and their son.

Copyright © 2015 by Disney Enterprises, Inc. and Pixar Animation Studios.
All rights reserved. No part of this book may be reproduced in any form without written permission from the publisher.

Slinky® Dog is a registered trademark of © POOF-Slinky, LLC

ISBN 978-1-4521-5505-0

Manufactured in the United States.

Design by Glen Nakasako, Smog Design, Inc.

10 9 8 7 6 5 4 3 2 1

Chronicle Books LLC
680 Second Street
San Francisco, California 94107

Chronicle Books—we see things differently.
Become part of our community at www.chroniclekids.com.

COOPER HEWITT

Cooper Hewitt,
Smithsonian Design Museum
2 East 91st Street
New York, NY 10128
cooperhewitt.org

Smithsonian Design Museum